TOP 10 HOCKEY HEROES

BY JON SCHER

The Child's World
childsworld.com

Published by The Child's World®
1980 Lookout Drive • Mankato, MN 56003-1705
800-599-READ • www.childsworld.com

Photo credits:
AP Photo: David Durochik 6; Fred Jewell 12; 14; John Swart 16; Ray Lussier/Boston Herald 19. Daily Dose 8. Dreamstime: Alexis Belec (cover), 1; Igor Mozjes 21; Getty Images: Denis Broderu/NHLI 15; Newscom: Archie Carpenter/UPI 7; Ezio Peterson 9; IHA/Icon SMI 10, 11; Jason Szenes/UPI Photo Service 13; Shelly Castellano/THN 17; IHA/Icon SMI 18.

ISBN: 9781503827288
LCCN: 2017960461

Printed in the United States of America
PA02380

CONTENTS

INTRODUCTION

WHO'S NUMBER ONE?

At the end of most hockey games, everyone knows who won. It's the team with the most goals! (Of course, sometimes it might also be a tie after regulation!)

At the end of the Stanley Cup playoffs, the No. 1 team is clear, too. It's the winner of the final game . . . and there's always a winner. So finding the top hockey team each season is easy. Choosing the greatest hockey player of all time is a bit harder. Is it the guy with the most goals? Or the player who was in the most games? Or is it the goalie who stopped the most shots? Fans, experts, and fellow players all have their opinions.

Opinions are different than facts. Facts are real things. Wayne Gretzky had 894 goals. That's a fact. Ice hockey is the greatest sport in the world. That's an opinion. The Montreal Canadiens have won a record 24 **Stanley Cups**.

Mario Lemieux

That's a fact. New York City's Madison Square Garden is the best place to watch a hockey game. That's an opinion.

Some people might think hockey is not that great. (I know: Can you believe it?) But that's fine; that's their opinion. However, they can't say "The Great One" didn't rack up those goals. That's a fact. Rangers fans think MSG is No. 1. But you would find a very different opinion in lots of other **rinks**, where fans think THEIR place is No. 1.

Wayne Gretzky

And that's where you come in. You get to choose who is the greatest hockey player ever. You will read lots of facts and stories about these great players. Based on that, what's your opinion? Who's No. 1? There are no wrong answers . . . but you might have some fun discussions with your hockey-loving pals! Then again, you might just pick the guy with the most goals . . . it's up to you!

Read on and then after you're done, make up your own Top 10 list.

JEAN BELIVEAU

MONTREAL CANADIENS

Maurice Richard scored more goals for Montreal. Guy Lafleur came along and scored more points. But no Montreal Canadiens player has ever been more admired than Jean Beliveau. The 6-3 center was a two-time NHL MVP. He led the league in goals twice and played in 13 All-Star games. When asked to describe Beliveau's greatness, players and fans point first to the way he played the game. He skated with confidence, power, and grace.

Beliveau was a great leader, too. He was the Canadiens captain for 10 seasons, the most ever. Beliveau's name is engraved on the Stanley Cup a record 17 times! Montreal won 10 Stanley Cup titles when he played. He was part of seven more seasons as a team manager.

The Montreal Canadiens have won 24 Stanley Cup championships in their history. That's 11 more than any other NHL team! Only the New York Yankees (27) have more titles in North American pro sports history.

NUMBERS, NUMBERS

Montreal All-Time Leaders

1. Guy Lafleur, 1,246 points
2. Jean Beliveau, 1,219 points
3. Henri Richard, 1,046 points

SIDNEY CROSBY

PITTSBURGH PENGUINS

The Pittsburgh Penguins have won the Stanley Cup five times since 1990. That's the most in that time.

Sidney Crosby's hockey career has been simply awesome. A native of Canada, he joined Pittsburgh in 2005. Since then, "Sid the Kid" has won, and won, and won some more. Crosby won the Hart Trophy as the NHL's MVP in 2007 and 2014. As captain of the Pens, he has lifted the Cup three times.

Want more winning? Nobody in hockey history owns more gold medals. Crosby captained Canada to a gold medal in the 2005 World Junior Championships (2005). He earned Olympic gold medals in 2010 and 2014. He helped Canada win the 2015 World Championship and the 2016 World Cup.

He did all that before he turned 30. Imagine what Crosby will do in the next 10 years!

NUMBERS, NUMBERS

Youngest NHL Scoring Champions

Player	Points	Season	Age
Sidney Crosby	120	2006-07	19
Wayne Gretzky	164	1980-81	20
Connor McDavid	100	2016-17	20

BOBBY HULL

CHICAGO BLACKHAWKS • WINNIPEG JETS

There was only one "Golden Jet." Bobby Hull got that nickname in part from his blonde hair. The "jet" part came from his amazing skating speed. He also had a powerful **slap shot**.

Hull was one of the flashiest and most successful players in hockey history. He led the Chicago Blackhawks to the 1961 Stanley Cup. Playing **center**, he won three NHL scoring titles and two MVP awards.

In 1972, the World Hockey Association was created as a rival to the NHL. Hull became the best player to jump to the new league. He got a $1 million bonus. That turned out to be a good deal! He scored 77 goals in 1974-75 for the Winnipeg Jets and led them two WHA titles.

The Hull family scored more goals than any other. Bobby scored 604 goals in his NHL/WHA career. His younger brother Dennis had 298, most for Chicago. Bobby's son Brett scored 527 goals in a 20-year career.

NUMBERS, NUMBERS

Chicago Blackhawks' all-time leading goal scorers

1. Bobby Hull, 604
2. Stan Mikita, 541
3. Steve Larmer, 406

MARK MESSIER

EDMONTON OILERS • NEW YORK RANGERS
VANCOUVER CANUCKS

How big a leader was the great Mark Messier? The NHL created a new award for leadership. They named it for him!

"Mess" won six Stanley Cups. The first four came in Edmonton when he teamed with Wayne Gretzky. Messier capped his career by leading the New York Rangers to the 1994 Cup title.

The Rangers hadn't won a Stanley Cup since 1940. Messier's fierce glare and tough play changed them. The team went from losers to winners. The Rangers trailed the New Jersey Devils 3-2 in the Eastern Conference finals. Messier promised that the Rangers would win Game 6. He scored three goals and they did! New York went on to win the Cup. Messier scored the Cup-**clinching** goal!

Messier is the only player to serve as captain for two different Stanley Cup-winning teams. He wore the "C" for the 1990 Oilers and 1994 Rangers.

NUMBERS, NUMBERS

Playoff Points: All-time Leaders

1. Wayne Gretzky, 382
2. Mark Messier, 295
3. Jari Kurri, 233

MAURICE RICHARD

MONTREAL CANADIENS

Maurice Richard was known as "The Rocket." He was that fast! The Rocket was quick and strong, with a powerful shot, too. Goalies never forgot "the Rocket's red glare." That was the fiery look in Richard's eyes when he tried to score. The Rocket was the first player ever to score 50 goals in a season. He was the first to reach 500 career goals, too. When he hung up his skates in 1960, his 544 career goals were the most ever. He was born and raised in Montreal. How perfect that he helped the hometown Canadiens win eight Stanley Cup titles! That included five in a row from 1956 to 1960.

People from Canada are Canadians. The hockey team is Canadiens, with an "e." That's because the word is spelled that way in French. Many people in Montreal speak French as well as English.

NUMBERS, NUMBERS

Rocket Richard scored 50 goals in 50 games during the 1943-44 season. Only four other NHL players have been able to match that: Mike Bossy, Wayne Gretzky, Mario Lemieux, and Brett Hull.

Roy used the "butterfly" style in goal. In this style, the goalie holds his glove and blocker wide, like wings. To block the puck, he drops to his knees.

PATRICK ROY

MONTREAL CANADIENS
COLORADO AVALANCHE

There's an old saying in the NHL: A hot goalie can carry a team to the Stanley Cup title. Over and over again, Patrick Roy (say "HRWAH"). proved the old saying is true. Roy was **in the net** when Montreal won in 1986 and 1993. He won two more Cups for the Colorado Avalanche in 1996 and 2001. The rock-solid goalie won the Conn Smythe Trophy as the playoff MVP in 1986. He was a 20-year-old **rookie**. In the playoffs, he gave up fewer than two goals a game. Roy later won two more Conn Smythe Trophies. He also won more playoff games than any other goalie. He was the guy you wanted in the net for every big game.

NUMBERS, NUMBERS

Goalies with Most Playoff Victories

1. Patrick Roy, 155
2. Martin Brodeur, 113
3. Grant Fuhr, 92

WAYNE GRETZKY

EDMONTON OILERS • LOS ANGELES KINGS
NEW YORK RANGERS

They called Wayne Gretzky "The Great One" for a reason. Lots of reasons, actually! Gretzky scored 894 goals, more than any other NHL player. He also had 1,963 assists, also tops in league history. He led the league in scoring 10 times. He won nine league MVP awards. Both are the most ever. He's also the only player ever to put up more than 200 points in a season. Of course, being The Great One, he did that four times!

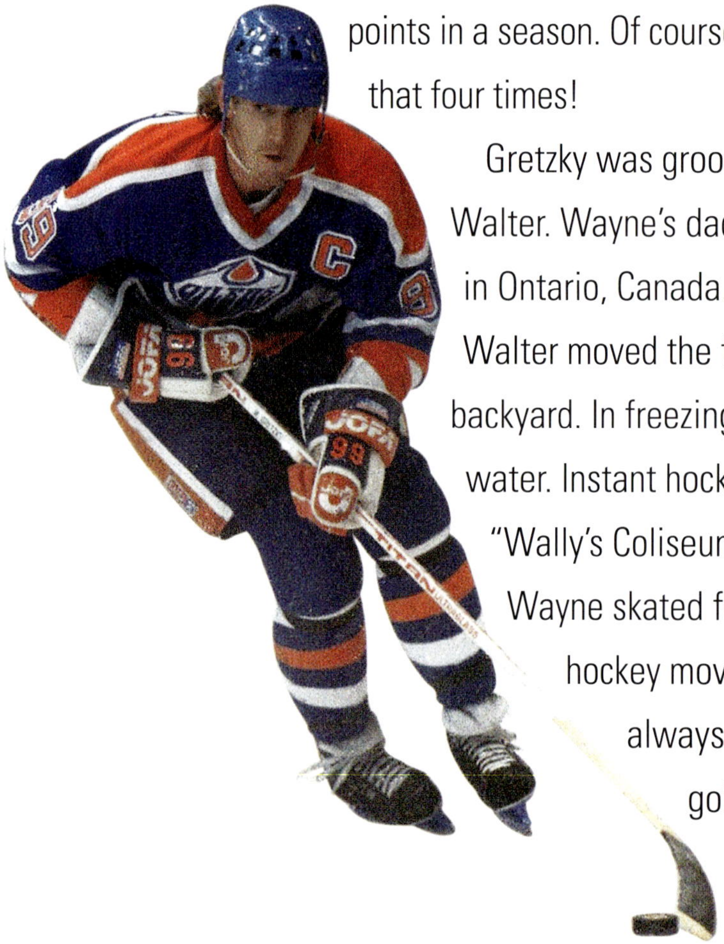

Gretzky was groomed for success by his father, Walter. Wayne's dad was a telephone repairman in Ontario, Canada. When Wayne was a baby, Walter moved the family to a house with a flat backyard. In freezing weather, he flooded it with water. Instant hockey rink! The kids called it "Wally's Coliseum." On the backyard **rink**, Wayne skated for hours. He practiced his hockey moves over and over. His father always said, "Go where the puck is going, not where it's been."

Wayne Gretzky won the Lady Byng Trophy five times. This award goes to very good players who also have great sportsmanship. Gretzky's Byng total was second-most ever.

Wayne was not a big kid. So he learned to skate and handle the puck well. With Walter's help, he became a **playmaker**. For example, he would take the puck behind the net. From there he looked for a teammate. Then, zing . . . a perfect pass! The area behind the net became known as "Gretzky's Office"!

Gretzky wasn't just the greatest goal scorer ever, he was a winner. He was the key player for the Edmonton Oilers in the 1980s. They won four Stanley Cups. Two times, Gretzky was the playoff MVP. In 1988, Gretzky was traded to the Los Angeles Kings. His superstar play helped make hockey popular in Southern California. He even led the Kings to the Stanley Cup Finals in 1993.

NUMBERS, NUMBERS

All-Time NHL Points Leaders

1. Wayne Gretzky, 2,857
2. Jaromir Jagr, 1,921
3. Mark Messier, 1,887

GORDIE HOWE

DETROIT RED WINGS • HOUSTON AEROS
HARTFORD WHALERS

They don't make players like Gordie Howe anymore! "Mr. Hockey" was one of the most skilled players ever to play pro hockey. He was also one of the toughest. He used his power and speed to score. He used his strength and his fists to strike fear into opponents.

Howe grew up in Saskatchewan, Canada. He quit school at 15 to work in construction and focus on hockey. At 18, he signed with the Detroit Red Wings in 1946. He became the only NHL player to play in five decades. The former teen star scored his last goal in 1980 for the Hartford Whalers. He was 52!

With Howe as their leader, the Red Wings won four Stanley Cup championships. They also finished first in the league seven straight years (1948–1955). Along the way, Howe was named NHL MVP six times. He led the league in scoring six times, too.

Howe played alongside his sons Mark and Marty for seven years in the WHA. He outscored them in six of those seasons!

In 1971, he retired for the first time. No one had scored more points. In 1973, he returned to the ice. The World Hockey Association started that year. The Houston Aeros convinced Howe to return. The trick? He got to play with his sons, Mark and Marty! Houston loved having all those Howes. They won two WHA championships together.

Gordie Howe finally hung up his skates for good in 1980.

Howe is fourth all-time with 1,850 points. He is first among fans as the all-time Mr. Hockey.

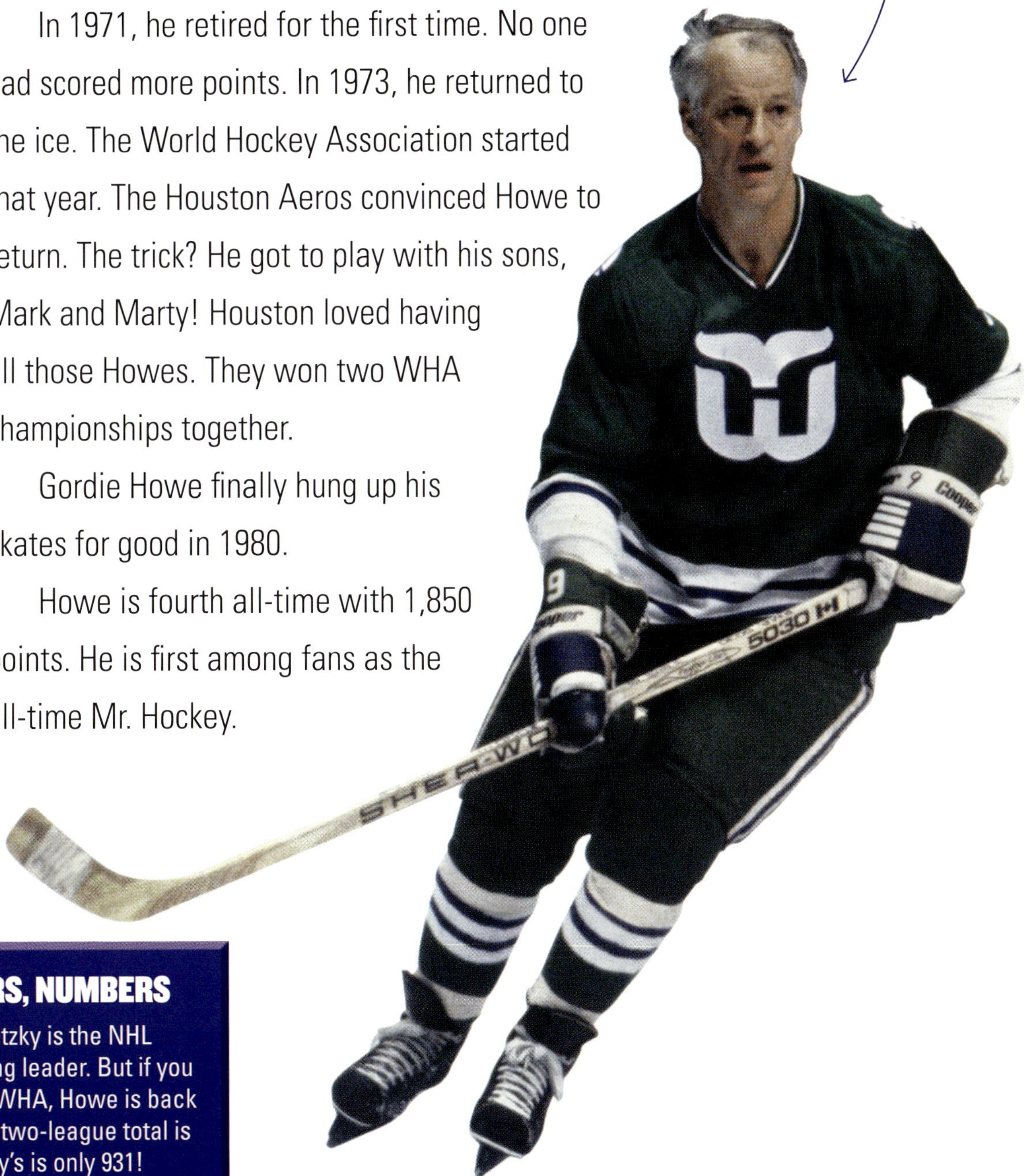

NUMBERS, NUMBERS

Wayne Gretzky is the NHL goal-scoring leader. But if you add in the WHA, Howe is back on top. His two-league total is 975. Gretzky's is only 931!

MARIO LEMIEUX

PITTSBURGH PENGUINS

Mario Lemieux is 6-4, which makes him the tallest player on this list. Put him in skates and he's 6-7! His height and his long arms let Lemieux simply reach around smaller players. It was almost unfair to the defense. He had his best season in 1988–89. Lemieux scored 85 goals and 199 points for Pittsburgh. That was one of six times he led the NHL in scoring.

Lemieux grew up in Montreal, Canada. He joined the Penguins as their top pick in the 1984 draft. The Penguins slowly built a championship team around him. They won back-to-back Stanley Cup titles in 1992 and 1993. Lemieux showed why he was called "Le Magnifique" in French. In English, he was "Super Mario."

During the 1993-94 season, Super Mario got very sick. He had a form of cancer. While he got better, he missed more than two months.

His comeback was amazing. Lemieux returned to lead the Penguins to 17 wins in a row. They set a team record with 119 points. He played two more seasons before retiring in 1997.

But he wasn't done. In 1999, he helped buy the Penguins. And he even played for five more seasons! He left the ice for good in 2006. Since then, as team owner, he has helped them win three more Stanley Cups!

Lemieux is the first former player to purchase an NHL team.

NUMBERS, NUMBERS

Pittsburgh Penguins' Top Goal Scorers

1. Mario Lemieux, 690
2. Jaromir Jagr, 439
3. Sidney Crosby, 397

BOBBY ORR

BOSTON BRUINS • CHICAGO BLACKHAWKS

It's the most famous photo in hockey history (at right). It shows Bobby Orr flying through the air like Superman. A second before, he had put puck in the net to win in **overtime**. The victory made his Boston Bruins the 1970 Stanley Cup champs! The photo also helps explain why Orr is one of the most important players in hockey history.

In the game, the Bruins and St. Louis Blues were tied 3-3 in OT. The Bruins' forwards were putting pressure on Blues goalie Glenn Hall. Suddenly Orr saw an opening. He sped up the ice. He took the puck on the right side and passed to Derek Sanderson behind the net. Orr then charged toward the goalie and tapped in a return pass from Sanderson! Gooooalll!

Orr turned the Bruins around. They had missed the playoffs eight years in a row. By his fourth season, they were Stanley Cup champs. Then they won again two years later! Boston didn't miss the playoffs again until 1997.

That's how Orr played the game. He was faster and stronger than other defensemen. He refused to sit back and just watch. Instead, Orr looked for moments to rush into the enemy zone. He created chance after chance for his team. His success on offense changed the way defensemen played. Still, nobody has ever done it better than Orr did. He is still the only defenseman ever to lead the NHL in scoring. And he did it twice!

Sadly, Orr had to retire at age 30 with knee injuries. His legend remains. So does that famous photo. In front of Boston's TD Garden, there's even a statue of Bobby Orr in midair!

NUMBERS, NUMBERS

Most points in a season by an NHL defenseman

Player	Season	Points
Bobby Orr	1970-71	139
Paul Coffey	1985-86	138
Bobby Orr	1974-75	135
Paul Coffey	1983-84	126
Bobby Orr	1973-74	122

YOUR TOP TEN!

In this book, we listed our Top 10 in no particular order. We gave you some facts and information about each player. Now it's your turn to put the players in order. Find a pen and paper. Now make your own list! Who should be the No. 1 hockey player of all time? How about your other nine choices? Would they be the same players as we chose? Would they be in the same order? Are any players missing from this book? Who would you include? Put them in order— it's your call!

Remember, there are no wrong answers. Every fan might have different choices in a different order. Every fan should be able to back up their choices, though. If you need more information, go online and learn. Or find other books about these great players. Then discuss the choices with your friends!

THINK ABOUT THIS . . .

Here are some things to think about when making your own Top 10 list:

- How much did he help his team?
- What were his greatest skills?
- Did his team win Stanley Cup titles?
- Why was he better than other players?

24

SPORTS GLOSSARY

blocker (BLOK-er) a wide pad worn on one of the goalie's arms, used to knock away hard shots

center (SENN-ter) a hockey position on offense that plays in the middle of the front line

clinching (KLINCH-ing) to get or to win something

in the net (IN THUH NET) hockey slang for playing goalie

overtime (OH-ver-tyme) extra hockey action played if the two teams are tied after the regulation 60 minutes

playmaker (PLAY-mayk-er) in hockey, a player who is great at setting his teammates up for shots on goal

rink (RINK) the name of any ice sheet on which hockey is played

rookie (ROOK-ee) a player in his or her first season of a pro sport

slap shot (SLAP SHOT) a play in hockey where the shooter takes a long backswing and whips his stick at the puck

Stanley Cup (STAN-lee KUPP) trophy given to the team that wins the National Hockey League championship; it is named for Canada's Lord Stanley, who donated the first cup in 1893.

FIND OUT MORE

IN THE LIBRARY

Herman, Gail. *Who Is Wayne Gretzky?* New York, NY: Penguin Workshop, 2015.

Hockey: From Then to Wow! Editors of Sports Illustrated Kids. New York, NY: Sports Illustrated Kids, 2017.

Leonetti, Mike. *A Hero Named Howe.* Vancouver, BC: Raincoast Books, 2006.

ON THE WEB

Visit our Web site for links about Top 10 hockey heroes: **childsworld.com/links**

Note to Parents, Teachers, and Librarians: We routinely verify our Web links to make sure they are safe and active sites. So encourage your readers to check them out!

INDEX

ABOUT THE AUTHOR

Jon Scher is a deputy editor at ESPN, where he's worked since 2000. As a writer-reporter at *Sports Illustrated,* he covered the NHL and wrote two cover stories on Mario Lemieux and the dominant Pittsburgh Penguins of the early 1990s. He lives in Brooklyn, NY, and has been rooting for the New York Rangers since before they won the Cup in 1994—really!